Mail Order

Millie

Widows, Brides, and Secret Babies

Cheryl Wright

Contents

MAIL ORDER MILLIE
(Widows, Brides, and Secret Babies)

Copyright ©2020by Cheryl Wright

Cover Artist: Black Widow Books

Dedication

To Margaret Tanner, my very dear friend and fellow author, for her enduring encouragement and friendship.

To Alan, my husband of over forty-six years, who has been a relentless supporter of my writing and dreams for many years.

To Virginia McKevitt, cover artist and friend, who always creates the most amazing covers for my books.

To You, my wonderful readers, who encourage me to continue writing these stories. It is such a joy knowing so many of you enjoy reading my stories as much as I love writing them for you.

Chapter One

Little Rock, Montana – 1880

Sheriff Cody Watson snatched up his wife and carried her lovingly across the threshold of their new home.

They'd met only four months ago, had a whirlwind courtship, and quickly married a month later. He had no intentions of letting this beauty get away.

He glanced down into her face. She appeared blissfully happy and he knew she was. She'd told him so at least twice a day. The thought made him smile.

They hadn't expected to be uprooted so soon after their marriage, but he'd been offered a position in the tiny outback town of Little Rock, and only a fool would say no.

The position came with a fully furnished house with no rent – all they had to do was bring their clothing. It suited him fine.

And Millie wasn't unhappy about the situation either. With both her parents dead after a stagecoach accident, there was nothing left in her hometown to stay for.

The job offer came with a bonus for the sheriff who could clean up the town and rid them of the Jonas Gang, who had been terrorizing Little Rock for some time. A huge bonus – one that would set them up for life.

He felt like a heel not telling Millie, but he didn't want his pretty little wife to worry. After all, he could handle himself. He'd put many a criminal behind bars already, so why should this gang be any different?

Millie leaned up and gently kissed his lips, then laughed, bringing him back to the present. Her voice tinkled when she laughed, and he never tired of hearing it. As her arms slid around his neck, he knew it was past time to get inside away from prying eyes.

He unlocked the front door, then kicked it open. He watched as Millie's eyes scanned the room. The house was far bigger than he'd expected, and it was detached from the sheriff's office. He liked that idea. It would keep Millie away from criminal types that might be in the jail.

Setting her gently to the floor, he leaned in and stole another kiss. Not just a gentle one either, this kiss sent a message. She didn't complain, but stared into his eyes. He could see the longing there, but they needed to unpack first.

Millie began to wander, exploring the place while he retrieved their luggage from outside the door.

"It's beautiful," Millie called from the bedroom, and he deemed to join her. Her hands meandered over the embroidered quilt that adorned the double bed they would share for as long they stayed in this cottage.

The action made him feel things he shouldn't be feeling. Especially in the middle of the day.

If he had his way, they would be here forever. It seemed a good place to bring up a family, but first he had to clean up the Jonas Gang. He would make it his mission to do so.

His heart hitched as Millie sat on the edge of the bed flashing a *come hither* look. He gently laid her down and began to undo those wretched buttons strewn down the back of her gown.

Millie stared down at her husband of a little less than three months. Three blissfully happy months.

Cody looked so peaceful lying there. His best suit fit perfectly and had always looked wonderful on him.

Her thoughts flashed back to their wedding day – the first day she'd seen him in that suit.

He was incredibly handsome standing beside her. His big brown eyes always drew her in, and those dimples. They always got to her.

And his lips. They were the most kissable lips she'd ever known. Not that she'd kissed any other man – that wouldn't be right – but Cody was a kisser if ever there was one.

They had big plans. They were going to build a house halfway up the mountain, despite the town supplying one.

He'd decided to get the money together for their own piece of land, and then they'd start building. She would help out where she could, perhaps selling baked goods to the local mercantile.

Their little bit of paradise would be large enough to house not only themselves, Cody had said, but their children. He'd planned on at least six. Millie preferred two or three. She would be the one caring for them after all.

She startled as the preacher came and stood beside her. "He was a wonderful man, Mrs Watson and we'll all miss him."

He shook his head and walked away, ready for the funeral service.

A tear slid down Millie's face as she pondered the preacher's words. She didn't know any of these people, and they didn't know her Cody. They had been here three days – not even long enough to unpack all their belongings.

Cody may not have been perfect, but he was her husband, and had always treated her well.

She stifled a sob.

"What am I going to do now, Cody?" she asked quietly, as the sob bubbled to the surface.

Out of nowhere the answer came to her in Cody's own voice. "Become a mail order bride."

"Are you crazy?" she asked out loud.

Heads turned to stare at her, and she felt the heat creep up her face. It was the craziest idea she'd ever heard, but it just might work.

~*~

Millie lay sleeping in the bed she'd shared with Cody for only a few days.

Her eyes fluttered open. She'd spent the days since Cody's death crying, and now they were red and sore.

Little did she know when they came here Cody was doomed. Not only was she mourning his death, but now she was furious with him. Why would he make a pact to wipe out a notorious gang knowing it could mean certain death?

She climbed out of bed and pulled back the curtains, looking out at the town she now hated with a vengeance.

Everyone was going about their every day business as though her husband hadn't lost his life. As though her world hadn't been turned upside down. And as though he hadn't tried to protect this sorry little town from the most ferocious criminals Cody had ever seen.

A sob bubbled up from her deep within her and she didn't even try to stifle it. The more she cried now, the easier it would be come. At least she hoped it would.

Millie pushed the curtains back in place and turned toward the kitchen. It was then the room began to spin. She reached out for the wooden chair that stood nearby. The chair that still held her dead husband's hat.

She looked down and sobbed. Again. Would she ever get over this loss?

Her head now settled, Millie ran to the privy as her stomach churned and threatened to empty. Any other time she'd be happy at this possible scenario. Cody had looked forward to the time they welcomed children into their lives.

As her mind ticked over, Millie stopped herself. This could just be a result of the turmoil she'd experienced over the past days.

She put her hands to her stomach. Surely she would know if she was with child? She swallowed hard, then shook her head.

No. She was not with child – it couldn't be. As much as she wanted Cody's child, she didn't want it without him.

As if by some miracle, the churning subsided, and she headed to the kitchen. She set two cups out for coffee, then realized her error. Would this torment never end?

There was a gentle knock at the door and brushing her tears away, she opened it gingerly.

The Mayor and his wife stood before her.

"Good morning Mrs Watson," the Mayor's wife said. "May we come in for a little chat?"

It was the last thing she needed right now, but Millie showed them into the sitting room, offering them coffee. "Let me help you," Mrs Dalton told her, and proceeded to prepare the drinks.

"How are you coping, my dear," she asked Millie gently, and Millie's eyes filled with tears. "Oh my dear girl," she said with real emotion in her voice. "Shall we sit down?"

They returned to the sitting room where the Mayor was waiting patiently. Millie swiped at her eyes and lifted her cup to her lips.

"The news isn't good, I'm afraid," Mayor Dalton told her gruffly.

"Abe, honestly!" his wife interjected. "The poor girl has just lost her husband." He threw his hands in the air.

"Perhaps you can do better," he said, then stormed out of the room. Millie heard the front door slam behind him.

Millie stared after him wondering what on earth was going on.

She glanced across at Mrs Dalton who's mouth was now drawn into a tight line. "Men!" she said, then leaned forward in her seat. "I'm sorry, Millie," she said gently, "But you have to leave here."

Her words might have been said as gently as possible, but the shock still set in. "L... leave?" Millie couldn't form any other words. She'd thought she would be able to stay for at least another few weeks. After all, her husband had just been murdered trying to save this town.

She felt Mrs Dalton's hand cover hers, but her brain was in a fog. Where would she go? How could she support herself? And if she was with child, which she thought was highly unlikely, how would she support her child?

She shook her head trying to clear the haze but it wasn't working. All she managed to do was make her head ache.

Millie began to stand in an effort to secure fresh air, and the room spun again. She slid slowly to the floor.

Chapter Two

Millie looked around at the meagre belongings she had. They were bagged up ready for the next leg of her journey – whatever that might be.

It was then the knock came at the door. Her greatest fear was she'd find Mayor Dalton standing there. His last visit didn't go so well.

She opened the door a crack, and stared at the stranger standing there. "Zachary Green, Ma'am," he said genially. "From the post office," he explained when she frowned.

Millie nodded.

"I have a telegraph for you, Ma'am." He handed the handwritten message over and left her alone. Nearly everyone had left her alone. She didn't know whether that was a good thing or not.

It had been difficult to comply with the Mayor's directive to leave within two weeks. A new sheriff was arriving with his wife shortly, he'd told her, and they needed the cottage.

Millie swallowed hard. Had the new sheriff's wife been warned? She was willing to bet she wasn't. Unfortunately she would likely be long gone before they arrived, so she'd have no opportunity to inform the poor woman of her destiny.

Her biggest wish was they didn't have children. It was hard enough for her, even childless.

She made her way to the sitting room and made herself comfortable on the embroidered and cushioned chair.

Mr Green had carefully folded the document into a small square before handing it over. She drew in her breath and began to open the thick paper, peering at the beautiful cursive writing.

She'd contacted a mail-order bride agency after being given her eviction orders by the Mayor. It was not a step she'd taken lightly, and she'd spent many a day praying to be sure it was the right thing to do.

Even so, she still wasn't convinced.

Due to the urgency of her situation, things had been hurried along. Hence the telegraph message she now held in her hands.

Her potential new husband instructed her to take the stage coach the next morning. It was fully paid for, and she was to collect a lump sum transferred to the local bank for her meals along the way and any other incidentals she may need.

Millie clutched at her chest. This surely couldn't be happening to her? She had recently buried one husband, and was about to marry another.

With both locations being in Montana, it would at least ease her inconvenience of traveling too far. Even if they were on opposite sides of the state.

She re-read the telegraph. Daniel Carson was her betrothed. She wondered what he would be like.

She had been shown a number of letters, and she'd chosen his. Out of all the potential husbands available, she'd chosen him.

He was far older than her twenty-six years, was almost thirty-two and owned his own business. She now wondered if his age would be a problem. Cody was closer to her age at twenty-eight.

But perhaps he was a little immature. One would certainly think so after learning of the ridiculous contract he'd taken out with the Little Rock Mayor.

She sighed, then checked all her belongings were packed and ready to go. Shoving the telegraph message into her pocket, Millie embarked on a rare visit outside the Sheriff's house.

Millie was relieved of her meagre belongings before she took the giant leap of entering the carriage. A young couple sat next to each other, hands entwined, staring lovingly at each other.

She stared at them for long moments, until she realized she likely appeared rude. They reminded her so much of herself and Cody.

She swallowed down her emotion when she understood this was exactly what they were like on their trip into Little Rock just weeks ago.

In only moments her life was in ruins. Her husband was shot dead, and her life was in turmoil. No matter how long ago it happened, she would never get over the sudden death of her beloved Cody.

She swallowed back a sob. This was neither the time nor the place. Besides that, she didn't want to make a spectacle of herself.

The carriage door was closed by the driver and she prepared for the arduous journey she anticipated. Suddenly the door was wrenched open and a disheveled cowboy joined them.

She straightened her shoulders and glanced across at him. How rude to have held up the other passengers. He didn't seem to care, and huddled down into the seat and pulled his hat down over his head.

The least she expected was an apology, but none was forthcoming. The young bride sitting opposite seemed equally aggravated at his rudeness.

Millie had worn her best gown in preparation of her forthcoming nuptials, but hadn't anticipated the dirt and the dust they would collect along the way. She brushed herself down at every stop. It was a good opportunity to clean herself off, albeit a little, and stretch her legs.

Thankfully, they stopped for nearly an hour at a number of towns along the way, allowing her to purchase food. She even managed a hot meal at the diner in a couple of places.

Her fellow passengers changed as the days rolled on, and the young couple had left them. No doubt to start their new lives together.

She envied them, and wished them well.

Despite the constant stomach churning rocking of the carriage, she managed to keep her food down.

She knew little of her betrothed except his name. Daniel Carson. She vaguely recalled he was involved with wood. Millie was still walking around in a haze, and her retention of information was not great. Hopefully it got better with time.

Already they'd traveled for three days – it could have been far worse. She anticipated the time when they arrived at Grand Falls. The driver told her it wasn't much further, when she'd asked. Her impression of *much further* could be far different to his, and she blanched at the thought.

Millie stared out the window as yet another town came into view. This one looked far bigger than any of the previous places they'd visited. Her heart pounded. Could her journey be at an end?

"Grand Falls," the driver shouted. "Grand Falls." He opened the door to the carriage and glanced at her. "This is your stop, Ma'am," he told Millie, and she was never so glad to see him.

She slowly stood, as much as she could, and thanked him. He took her hand and helped her down the rickety steps.

She stood on the wooden side-walk and looked around. Grand Falls was far bigger than she'd anticipated. Which could only be a good thing, right?

At least she convinced herself of that fact.

She watched as a well-dressed man rushed across the dusty road toward the stage coach. He was a handsome man, though no one would ever compare to her Cody. His dark hair flicked across his eyes as he rushed, and he brushed it back with his fingers.

His piercing blue eyes never left her face.

"Miss Watson? Millie?" he asked when he was face-to-face with her.

She stopped brushing the dust from her gown, and straightened her shoulders. "I am Millie Watson," she said. "I assume you are Mr Carson?"

He shoved his hand toward her. "Daniel Carson. Very pleased to meet you."

She accepted his hand and winced at his strength, then jerked her hand away.

The smile left his face. "I'm sorry, Ma'am. I don't know my own strength sometimes." He leaned down and picked up the luggage at her feet.

"Once we have all your luggage, we'll head to the church. The preacher is waiting."

She felt the heat creep up her neck and into her cheeks. She averted her eyes. "That's all my luggage," she said, fully embarrassed. "Things have been rather difficult."

And they had. Since her parents had died she was lucky to have survived. With no known family, she was plucked off the streets by Cody's parents. That was how they met.

What she would have done otherwise, she'd never know. The mere thought of Cody had her emotions high, and her eyes filled with tears.

She turned away so her potential husband would not discover her weakness.

He didn't look happy, but put his arm around her shoulders and led her away from the small group milling around the stage coach. Was it only to stop his own embarrassment?

Once out of sight, he reached into his pocket and handed her his kerchief. She glanced up at him. "I'm sorry," she said. "It's been a very emotional few weeks." She wiped at the tears that wouldn't stop falling.

He raised an eyebrow. "No need to apologize," he said gently, then led her toward a large building not far away. He shoved the door open and guided her inside.

"Mrs Francis," he called to an unseen woman. She scurried at his voice.

She glanced across at Millie but didn't comment on her presence. "Can you organise a strong coffee for Millie, please?"

He sat her down, and placed the luggage behind her desk. "When you feel up to it, we'll head over to the church."

She nodded and accepted the coffee. "Thank you," she said meekly and took a sip, then upon finding it wasn't glaringly hot, took a larger mouthful.

Millie stared at her future husband over the mug. He'd pulled a chair from behind the large mahogany desk to sit opposite her.

That was surely better than glaring at her from behind the big desk. "Feeling better?" He looked genuinely concerned, but also seemed somewhat impatient. He likely had things to attend to, and Millie was impeding his plans.

She nodded, which had him smiling. "Mrs Francis," he called again. "Please show Millie where she can get cleaned up." He stood and Millie took it as being her cue to also stand.

She followed the indefinable Mrs Francis out to a back room. She couldn't wait to get clean water on her face. She might finally feel normal again.

Daniel watched as Millie followed Mrs Francis out to the back room. He was aware she'd been in difficult circumstances recently, but nothing more.

He didn't however expect her to be in such a depressive state. He wondered if they should put the wedding off until she felt better able to cope?

He'd applied for a mail-order bride some time ago, but he'd not found anyone suitable to date. When an urgent telegraph arrived from the agency, he knew it was time he stopped dilly-dallying around.

The poor woman needed help, and needed it quickly. He was more than willing to help, as it would assist them both.

He took a deep breath and let it out slowly. Sometimes he was his own worst enemy.

Daniel glanced up as she entered the room again. With her face cleaned and her blonde hair tied back, she looked far more presentable than when he'd collected her from the stagecoach.

He stared at her, then grinned. "You look far happier now," he said. "A good clean up can do wonders."

"I do feel better," she said. "I'm ready when you are."

Mrs Francis glanced across at him quizzically. He hadn't told the woman his plans – it was none of her business – but conceded he would have to tell her sometime.

"I'll be back later," he told her, daring her to question him. As predicted, she said not a word, but closed the door quietly behind them.

Daniel offered his arm to the beautiful woman standing beside him. She took it graciously.

Now that he could see her face more clearly, he noticed she had a glow about her. More likely than not it was exhaustion. The poor girl had been in that wretched stagecoach for days.

"Oh," she said suddenly, reaching for her reticule. "I have your leftover money. I did appreciate it very much," she said quietly. "I don't know what I would have done otherwise.

He waved her away. "You keep it. Use it to buy something for yourself."

"But..."

"Honestly, keep it." Did she really think he was desperate for the few coins that would still be available?

She nodded. He could see she was lost. It was almost as though her brain was in a haze, and he belatedly wondered if a nap might do her some good.

"Ah, here we are at the church. The preacher may have given up on us by now." He grinned, then winked at her, trying to lighten the mood a little, but it didn't seem to help her demeanor at all.

When they reached the front of the church, she stopped suddenly and closed her eyes. If he didn't know better he'd think she was having second thoughts.

"Millie?" She didn't answer and he tried again. "Millie? Is everything alright?"

At the sound of her name she opened her eyes and glanced at him. "I'm fine, thank you," she answered, but it was very obvious she was not alright.

"Shall we sit at the back of the church for a moment or two? Give you a chance to compose yourself?"

She glared at him briefly, then her face softened. Did she understand he was trying to help her?

He reached for the door, but it was opened for him. Preacher Angus Devon stood before them, a grin on his face.

"Welcome, welcome!" he said, more than a little animated. He'd told Daniel how pleased he was that he was finally getting hitched. "And this must be the happy bride?"

He stepped back and realization was written all over his face. "Come my dear," he said gently. "You wait here, Daniel, while Millie and I have a little talk."

He watched as the pair walked down the aisle and sat on the front pew. He could hear mutterings, but nothing discernable, and Millie bowed her head, shaking and nodding now and then.

If anyone could console her it was Preacher Devon. Daniel had known him most of his life. The man had seen him through his desperation when Alison had been killed.

Daniel bowed his head and prayed. He prayed for the Lord to bring peace to his new bride.

When he looked up, the preacher was beckoning for him to join them out the front. He was holding Millie's hand, patting it as if to comfort her.

She glanced up as he approached. "I'm ready now," she said softly, and turned toward the front of the church, studying the stained glass window.

The preacher passed her hand over to him.

Her skin was soft and warm, and her hands small. He stared at her profile. He could imagine waking up to her beautiful face for the rest of his life.

"Are you ready, Daniel?"

He turned to Millie and she nodded. "Yes, Preacher Devon," he said, his voice a little shaky.

"We are gathered here today..."

Daniel heard movement behind him and glanced over his shoulder. Mrs Devon and Mrs Highmont – the regular witnesses – had taken their place on the front pew.

The ceremony was over as quickly as it had started, and all that was left was to sign the marriage certificate.

He turned to Millie. She smiled when she noticed him watching her, but she didn't seem genuinely happy. He leaned in and whispered in her ear. "It's not too late to back out."

She refuted his concerns. "I'm perfectly fine," she said, but he wasn't convinced.

They thanked the preacher and left.

She hooked her arm through his, and they returned to his office to collect her belongings. He would then escort her home.

It had already been a very long day. He could only hope it got better.

Chapter Three

Millie glanced around trying to get a feel for where everything was.

As she looked back, she spotted the building Daniel had taken her to. In big black letters it told her all she needed to know: Carson Saw Mills.

Her husband *owned* the saw mill. At least he wasn't the sheriff. She wouldn't survive another loss like she'd recently endured.

A shiver went down her spine.

"We're home."

His words cut through her thoughts, and she looked at the building standing before her. It wasn't a mansion, but it certainly wasn't a cottage either.

She'd been more than happy with the sheriff's cottage in Little Rock, but what stood before her now was more than she had ever imagined.

But it didn't feel like home.

Daniel turned the key in the door, then whisked her off her feet and into his arms. She stared at him momentarily, then pressed her face into his shoulder. She could hear his heart beating fast. Every bit as fast as hers.

She breathed deeply trying to get the essence of her husband, but he wasn't Cody.

For a moment she'd forgotten. Pushed the heartache to the back of her mind. Trying to forget had helped her survive this far, but going forward it wouldn't work. Millie knew it wouldn't.

Was it really only weeks since Cody had carried her across the threshold in Little Rock? She stifled a sob.

She felt her new husband stiffen. "Are you alright?" he asked quietly.

She swallowed and lifted her head, planting a false smile on her face. "Perfectly," she lied.

He stepped into the sitting room and placed her gently on the floor. "Well, this is it," he said. "Welcome home."

Home. Was it really?

She looked about. The room was chilly, and she rubbed at her arms.

He watched her every movement, then squatted in front of the fire. "Let me light this," he said, adding twigs and newspaper to the empty fireplace. "I usually put it on when I get home at night."

She nodded then went looking for the kitchen. It appeared to be well-equipped, and she could feel the warmth from the wood stove.

Opening the door she discovered it needed topping up. Millie did what was needed, then filled the kettle and placed it back on the stove.

"Would you like coffee," she asked stiffly, as he entered the kitchen. "I've refueled the stove."

He shook his head. "I have to get back to the office," he said. "Is that a problem?"

She should have realized. She had caused him enough inconvenience for one day.

"Millie," he said as he began to leave. "We will eat out tonight – to celebrate our marriage." He walked back to her and looked as though he wanted to hug her, but held back. They were, after all, total strangers. "I know things are difficult now, but we'll work it out."

She stared at him and more than anything, needed to be hugged. She melted into his arms. Pretending he was Cody wasn't going to help in the long term, but right now it was what she needed. Wanted.

Her arms snaked up around his back, and he gingerly lifted his arms and enveloped her. She wondered how he would feel if he knew what she'd been thinking. She felt terrible about her absolute deception, and let her arms drop to her sides, then stepped back. "Don't let me keep you," she said, no longer able to look him in the eye.

He stared down at her, confused. "Explore, put your things away if you feel up to it. Maybe take a nap. You've had a big day."

He hugged her again, briefly this time, then strolled out the door and out of sight.

Millie felt ashamed. How could she do such a thing? Let him think she was hugging him when in her mind it was her dead husband?

Daniel had been nothing but kind to her, and this was how she repaid him. Butterflies churned in her stomach. She ran through the house looking for the bathroom. She found it only moments before her stomach emptied.

Tears flooded her face. What was Daniel going to say? He didn't sign up for another man's child.

She took a steadying breath. She could be totally wrong. Perhaps it was the long and rocky trip making her feel ill.

Yes, that was it. Millie smiled, glad she'd settle that.

Millie found the master bedroom and hung her few gowns in the wardrobe there. She'd located an empty draw and added her undergarments.

Then she drew a bath.

It was good to wash the dust and grime away, and to feel clean again. She even managed to wash the grit from her hair.

Her eyes closed, she relished the opportunity to just lay there and not think about the world around her. It felt like she'd soaked in the warm water forever.

There was a quiet tap on the door and her eyes fluttered open. Surely Daniel couldn't be home already?

"Millie? Are you alright?"

She reached for a fluffy white towel. The water was only lukewarm now anyway. "I'm fine," she called back. "Thought I'd better clean up."

She wrapped the soft towel around herself and stood in the bath, not wanting to move, but knew she had to. "How much longer do I have?"

There was no answer. He'd obviously gone, which suited her fine. Millie hadn't taken the time to think much before, she'd been so exhausted, and just wanted to relax.

The soaking had done her good, and she really enjoyed it, but it would have been nicer with some fragrant bubbles.

She gasped – she'd never thought like that before. Why was she starting now?

Because her new husband was obviously well off? What a terrible thing to think. Now she felt really bad, and vowed not to think like that again.

Once dry, she took her time dressing. First impressions count, and she wanted to give Daniel a good first impression of her.

She'd chosen her favorite gown. It wasn't expensive, and it wasn't covered in embroidery like the more fashionable ladies were wearing these days. But it was functional, and it was pretty, even if it was a little threadbare.

She gazed at the garment draped over the chair and had second thoughts. Would this gown embarrass her husband? Would he be annoyed that she'd arrived with few clothes and low-grade ones at that?

"Are you nearly ready, Millie?" His muffled voice came through the thick door.

"Coming." She opened the door and stood before him, and his eyes opened wide.

"You look beautiful," he said, his eyes simmering.

She turned around to have her back to him. "Would you mind fastening the gown for me?" It seemed a little forward to ask this so soon in their relationship, but he was her husband, and she couldn't do it herself.

His hands hovered over her shoulders. For a moment she wasn't convinced he was going to do it. Almost as though he was afraid to touch her.

Finally he lowered them to her shoulders and leaned in. "You smell like the lavender bush out the front," he said quietly.

She laughed. "I hope you don't mind – I threw some lavender buds into the bath. I love the fragrance, and it helps relax me."

"I don't mind at all," he said softly, his lips hovering over her neck.

Millie turned her head slightly to look at him. "Are you going to fasten my gown?" Her request was gentle, not forceful at all. He quirked an eyebrow. "My back is getting cold."

He laughed, and Millie enjoyed the sound. It was very masculine, and she could get very used to it.

After he'd secured her gown, he turned her around to face him. "You certainly are a beauty, Millie. I'm so lucky to have you as my wife."

She felt the heat creep up her face.

Until now she'd been apprehensive. She had no idea what sort of man she would end up with. Becoming a mail-order bride was very risky. She'd heard stories of women who had been bashed and abused, some even killed by their husbands.

She was certain Daniel was not like that.

"I've stoked the fire, so if you're ready we can go," he said, hooking her arm through his.

He looked very smart in his suit, and she was proud to call him her husband.

He soon led her outside and they made their way to the diner. Mrs Baker was the owner, he'd told her, and was the best cook in town. Although these days she did have help as not only was she getting older, but Grand Falls was getting bigger. Her business was also growing.

Millie lifted her skirts as they walked up the few steps and onto the side-walk. She'd never lived in such a big town as this.

Or rather, as Daniel had informed her as they headed to the diner, Grand Falls was a city. And one day it would be even bigger, and his business would grow.

New settlers would need timber for their homes and buildings. He was adamant about it.

Of course that meant more money. The one thing she and Cody had lacked was money. The love was there, but they skimped on everything because a sheriff's wage was very little. Hence the reason they were so grateful to get a house rent-free.

"Here we are," Daniel said, breaking into her thoughts. She'd been far away and hadn't heard another word he said.

"Good evening, Daniel." The older woman greeted him like she knew him well.

"Mrs Baker, I'd like to introduce you to my wife, Millie." He grinned, indicating he seemed happy about their union. Or perhaps he just liked the thought of it?

"Oooh, I'm very pleased to meet you, Millie." She reached for Millie's hands and squeezed them. "The poor girl is freezing, Daniel. What is wrong with you, bringing her out like this?" She scowled at him, and Millie felt the heat creep up her face.

He touched her bare arms. "Millie, I'm sorry. I didn't think," he said, removing his jacket and draping it over her shoulders.

"I'll put you next to the fireplace. Follow me."

When they were seated and left alone, she tried to apologize. "It's my fault, not yours," she said, but he was having none of it.

"You're new in town, I should have ensured you were probably attired."

Mrs Baker suddenly appeared and handed them each a menu. "Here are the menus," Mrs Baker said, smiling across at her. "We have a good range. You should find something you like." In a flash she was gone.

"Don't be too slow making a decision. If I know Mrs Baker, she'll be back before we know it." She glanced up at him, and he was grinning. "The old girl gets a tad impatient," he said.

It seemed like only moments later when she was back again.

Millie's eyes scanned the menu. "Beef and vegetable soup and warm bread please, Mrs Baker," she said when asked.

Daniel scowled. "That's not enough, surely."

"It's been a long day, Daniel. I don't feel like eating much."

He nodded. "Plus you've likely been tossed about most of that time, I'm certain." He turned to the older woman. "Sirloin for me please, Mrs Baker."

"For something different," she said, then laughed. "He always orders sirloin," she told Millie conspiratorially then left them alone.

The meal was lovely – the best Millie had consumed for ages, and she told their hostess. "You can bring her again, Daniel," Mrs Baker said, patting the younger woman's hand.

They had apple pie and clotted cream for dessert and they each had coffee.

She wasn't sure if it was the food, the heat from the fire, or exhaustion from the long trip she'd recently endured, but Millie had a hard time staying awake.

She felt Daniel's eyes on her, and was consumed with embarrassment. "I'm really sorry," she told him quietly.

He stood, scraping his chair along the floor. "Don't apologize," he said. "I've been selfish. I should have realized you needed to sleep."

She was too tired to argue, and welcomed his help getting to her feet.

He paid the bill, which Mrs Baker insisted was on the house, but he wouldn't accept, then helped Millie into his jacket.

At the back of his mind was that perhaps she didn't have a warm coat, and made a mental note to organise one for her.

"I had a wonderful time," she said as they farewelled Mrs Baker.

"We'll see you next time," Daniel said. "When Millie is not so tired."

The cold air hit her in the face as they stepped outside, and helped to wake her up somewhat, but not enough. She still needed sleep.

A soft mattress, a comfortable pillow, and warm coverings, that's what she needed. And that's exactly what Daniel told her she would have.

Daniel made himself scare while Millie prepared for bed. They'd not broached the subject of where they would each sleep – they were man and wife, and so he would assert his right to sleep with his wife.

He wouldn't pressure her into having relations with him. They were complete strangers. He wanted to get to know her first, and he was certain she would want to do that too.

He pushed the embers around the wood stove and threw more wood in it. Then he filled the kettle. It was a routine he'd followed all his years of living alone, and was something he'd watched his mother do when he was a child.

Then he went to the sitting room and did something similar. Keeping the house warm overnight had become a ritual as well.

He much preferred the warmer weather, and wasn't at all keen on the cold and especially the snow when it came.

He sat down on one of the padded chairs and reached for his bible. He read a passage every night, and it never failed to comfort him.

They hadn't discussed it, but he hoped Millie was a Christian woman. He felt certain she would be.

When he finished reading, he closed his bible. It had been his grandfather's and was rather tattered around the edges, but Daniel treasured it, and wouldn't be replacing it any time soon.

He never would, if he had his way. It was something he'd want to pass onto his own children one day.

That made him pause. One day he and Millie would have a family of their own. At least he hoped they would.

He stared out the window at the dark sky and the stars. What an extraordinary day he'd had. When he awoke this morning, he was a bachelor, and now he was a married man.

And to a beautiful woman no less.

He padded down to the bathroom and had a quick wash, then went to the bedroom. He'd expected to find Millie wide awake. Over tiredness can do that to you, he knew, but she was sound asleep.

He quietly changed into his nightgown and neatly folded his clothes, placing them on the chair. He then climbed into bed.

She didn't so much as flinch.

He knew this day would come, the day he married, but he hadn't expected it quite so soon.

He stared into her face – she was a stunner. He'd have to keep an eye on some of those young bucks in town. They'd try to steal her in a flash.

He was certain Millie wouldn't be willing. At least he hoped she wouldn't. She had a stable life with him, and he was glad to have her in it.

As he lay in the bed next to her, Daniel watched her breathe, her chest rose and fell gently, and he was tempted to touch her. He reached out his hand to stroke her cheek, but quickly pulled it back.

There was plenty of time for that. First he needed to get to know her, and she needed to get to know him.

He lay there staring, and was soon fast asleep.

Chapter Four

Millie awoke a little after dawn. She'd been doing it for so long, she couldn't get out of the habit.

As she slid out of bed, she noticed Daniel sound asleep on the other side. She'd assumed they would sleep in separate beds until they got to know each other. It was too late now.

She'd needed that sleep to replenish her energy. She'd been fine until dessert arrived, and then exhaustion had hit her.

At least Daniel wasn't angry with her. He seemed to take it in his stride.

She stood watching him peacefully sleeping for a few minutes, then headed to the kitchen to prepare her husband's breakfast.

She checked the pantry and found some thick cut bacon, bread, eggs, butter, and milk. There were also some canned beans.

She sliced the bacon thinly and threw it into to the frying pan with some lard. She mixed the eggs and milk to make scrambled eggs and added them to a pot. Lastly she toasted some of the bread in the wood stove.

By the time he had arisen and come to the kitchen, Daniel's breakfast was ready.

He stood in the doorway and breathed deeply. "That smells amazing," he said, then strolled over to Millie and kissed her cheek – as though it was the most natural thing in the world to do. He moved closer and put his arms around her, pulling her closer.

She enjoyed the hug, she truly did, but reluctantly shrugged out of his grip. "Your breakfast will be ruined," she said, indicating for him to sit at the table.

He'd not long sat when his meal was placed in front of him. Millie poured them both a mug of coffee.

Once she sat, he reached for her hands and bowed his head in prayer. "Thank you, Lord, for this meal, and for sending Millie to me. Amen."

He tucked in. "Thank you for a delicious breakfast, Millie," he said between mouthfuls. "I haven't eaten breakfast for months."

She stared at him. "My goodness," she said. "That changes now."

He grinned at her, and it set her heart on fire.

Daniel finished his food and placed his plates in the sink. "I have to go," he said, pulling on his jacket. "Go to the Mercantile and get yourself a coat, and anything else you need, and put it on my account."

She shook her head. "I don't need anything." She had only just arrived. She had no intention of costing her husband money this early in the game.

He stared at her. "Where is your warm coat, Millie?" he said firmly. She bit at her lip. Her only coat was far from warm. "I thought so. I'll let them know you're coming. You'll probably need to buy food too."

She followed him to the front door where he glanced at the coat rank. "I expect to see your coat here when I return."

He gently lifted her chin and moved in close. She stared up at him. Was he going to kiss her?

She swallowed.

Daniel's lips caressed hers. His kiss was a soft as a kitten's fur, and her lips tingled from where they'd connected. She felt like a swooning teenager.

"I'll see you at lunch," he whispered, and then he was gone.

The moment the door closed, she swung into action – she had a long list of things to do today.

First she dressed, then washed the dishes and cleaned up the kitchen. Then she checked the pantry.

It really was in a sorry state. Millie made a list of the staple items she needed, then worked out her meal plan for the next couple of days. That way she could pick up all the necessary items at the Mercantile today.

She really dreaded going there, knowing it was going to cost Daniel a lot of money. And all because of her.

Her list complete, including a warm coat, Millie went to make the bed. She leaned over and pulled the sheets into place, then straightened the covers.

As she stood up, her head spun, forcing her to sit on the side of the bed. It was obvious she was still suffering from exhaustion. She felt sure her sleep last night would have cured her of that.

She wouldn't tell Daniel – he might worry.

As soon as the room settled around her, she checked the wood stove and fire were fully fueled, then looked about for a basket. There was none to be found, likely as there had been no women in the house. At least she assumed that to be the case.

It wasn't long before she was able to wander over to the Mercantile. She passed Daniel's building on her way, and glanced across at the office, but couldn't see him. Not that she'd expected to.

The Mercantile was large. She'd never seen one that big before, but Grand Falls was a city, so she guessed that was the reason. It would surely be busy.

And it was. There were more than a dozen customers inside, all perusing the goods displayed on the shelves.

"Hello, Millie."

It was a familiar voice, and she spun around to see Mrs Baker standing next to her. "Oh, hello, Mrs Baker. I've come to do some shopping." She pulled out her list. "Daniel has little in his pantry," she whispered conspiratorially.

Mrs Baker laughed. "Why am I not surprised." She wandered off to do her own shopping.

Millie found a rack of warm coats and flicked through them. She checked the price tag of each and decided they were far too expensive, and began to walk away.

She heard the front door open and spun around to see her husband strolling toward her. "Good," he said. "Which one are you getting?" He pulled an expensive looking coat off the rack.

"I... how did you know I was here?" She felt annoyed. Didn't he trust her to get a coat? Then she heated. She'd already rejected them before he arrived.

"I saw you walk by my office." He lifted the coat and held it against her. "What do you think, Mrs Baker?" he called from across the shop. The older woman came rambling across.

She shook her head. "This one is far prettier."

The coat she held was made of beige wool and had panels that made it look more feminine. It had deep pockets either side, where Millie could put her kerchief and other items she might want to conceal.

At the shoulders, the sleeves ruffled, and the back was gathered below the shoulders.

Daniel stared at the coat in question. "It certainly is pretty. Will it be warm enough?"

Mrs Baker shoved the garment toward him. "Just feel the quality. It is very thick, and should last for many years."

"Oh, but it's so expensive!" Millie blanched at the price tag, and backed away.

"We'll take this one, Jacob," he called to the Mercantile owner. "But my wife will be wearing it home." The decision had been taken out of her hands.

The store owner nodded, and took the price tag Daniel handed over to him. "Add this and anything else Millie needs to my account, won't you?"

He'd effectively introduced her to the Mercantile owner, and authorized her to put whatever she wanted on his account. It made Millie feel slightly better.

Her husband helped her into the new wool coat he'd just paid a fortune for. She felt more than a little guilty at wasting his hard earned money, but it was certainly warm and comfortable.

"Perhaps Mrs Baker might help you select some new gowns and, er, unmentionables, and anything else you need." He had the decency to blush, then leaned in and kissed her cheek as though he'd done it a hundred times before. "I must return to work now. I'll see you at lunch."

"But Daniel..." Too late, he was gone.

Mrs Baker took her by the arm. "Come on, we have instructions to spend your husband's money." The older woman was grinning. "Oh, lighten up, Millie," she said when Millie stood there stony-faced. "It's not often you get to splash out on clothes."

She looked Millie up and down and moved in close. "How many gowns do you own?" Her voice was low in an obvious attempt not to embarrass her.

"Three, including this one." It was difficult to admit such a thing, and it was apparent as Daniel's wife she would not be allowed to parade around town in such threadbare garments.

She grabbed Millie's arm and took her to a corner in the back of the store. "Pick out three gowns for everyday wear, some nightgowns, and a robe. We'll visit the dressmaker for your other gowns."

Millie's mouth opened in disbelief. "I can't do that. Daniel would have conniptions!"

"Three gowns – go on." She stared Millie down, daring her to refuse. When she didn't choose for herself, Mrs Baker chose for her.

Millie clutched onto her shopping list, her stress levels getting higher by the moment.

"Daniel is not a stingy man, Millie," she said quietly. "Nor is he poor – far from it. He wants to look after you, and that includes outfitting you in a fashion that is indicative of being his wife."

They took the gowns and other items required, including several sets of unmentionables, and they were added to Daniel's account.

Mrs Baker walked with her out onto the side-walk. "I have to organize luncheon at the diner, but I can pick you up at two-thirty if you're free?"

Millie stared at her. Two-thirty? What was that about? "I..."

"We'll visit the dressmaker and have you properly outfitted."

She leaned in and hugged Millie. "I like you, my girl," she said convincingly. "We're going to be good friends, I can just feel it." Still a little shell-shocked at everything that had happened the last couple of days, Millie stared after her as she headed toward the diner.

Warm and snug in her new coat, she stared down at the huge package in her arms. *What on earth was Daniel going to say?*

~*~

Daniel stood in the doorway and breathed in the enticing aroma coming from the kitchen.

His house had become a home within only one day of Millie arriving. What would it be like when she'd been here a week, or a month? Or even a year?

He cleared his throat, not wanting to scare her, since she obviously hadn't heard him come in.

She spun around to stare at him, her hands to her chest. "I didn't know you were home," she said breathlessly.

"From now on, you lock the front door," he said gently. "You don't know who might wander in."

She laughed. "Such as the likes of you?"

She looked more rested today, but was still a little pale. He hoped she took the time to rest today.

"Lunch is almost ready. Sit down and I'll serve it shortly." She placed a mug of coffee in front of him, and set the cutlery and napkins on the table. "Have you had a good day so far," she asked.

Was she genuinely interested, or playing the part of the good wife? "It's been busy but good. How did your shopping go?"

She turned to stare at him. "Mrs Baker insisted I get three gowns. That is far too much."

Only three? "It's nowhere near enough. You need to go back for more."

Millie put her hands on her hips and stared at him. "She says she's taking me to the dressmaker this afternoon. Daniel, I..."

"Good. You need clothes, and I need you to dress appropriately." He frowned. "Have you never attended balls or galas? As my wife you will attend many functions over time."

She stared down at the floor. "I've never been to any of those things." She looked deflated, like she'd let him down.

Daniel shoved his chair back to stand in front of her. He gently lifted her chin with his fingers. "It's perfectly fine," he said, brushing her lips with his. "It will be fun. You'll see."

He leaned over to look into the pan. "Fried potatoes?"

"With pancakes, onion, and bacon," she said, opening the oven door.

He could certainly get used to this.

Millie was finishing up preparing supper when Mrs Baker arrived.

She pulled off her apron and hung it on the door.

"Come in," she said, opening the door wider. She was still quite concerned about spending all this money, despite what Daniel had told her.

"What did that handsome husband of yours say about your new clothes?" Mrs Baker had a twinkle in her eye as though something untoward had occurred.

Millie stared at her. "Not a lot. But he did agree with you about the dressmaker." She sighed, still not convinced. "He said I would have to attend functions and balls and such."

"Of course." The other woman's face lit up. "I wish my dear Harold had been interested in such things. Now that he's gone, I've no one to take me. Besides," she said, tugging at her scarf. "I don't have the time these days. I have a business to run."

Millie wasn't sure how to respond, so nodded.

"Right then my girl, grab your coat and off we go."

She helped Millie into her coat, and they headed toward the dressmaker's shop. It was on the main street, but much further along than the diner. Millie was agog at the variety of stores Grand Falls had. They even had a shoe shop and a millinery.

"We'll need to visit there too," Mrs Baker said gently. "You will be expected to dress to the nines for some of the functions. They're high fashion, you know."

No, Millie did not know, and she was disliking the idea more and more. But there was an expectation of her accompanying her husband to these distasteful functions, so go she must.

She cringed inwardly.

"Ah, here we are."

Upon noticing the two women entering the store, Joseph Harkley sprinted toward them. "Good afternoon Mrs Baker. And who is this delectable creature you have with you?"

He was charming, she would give him that. "I am Mrs Daniel Carson. Millie," she said firmly. It sounded strange, after finally becoming used to being Mrs Cody Watson.

"Millie here needs clothes for the functions she will attend."

He raised an eyebrow, then rubbed his hands together. Millie was sure he was clicking the dollar signs over in his mind.

"Joe will look after you, Millie," Mrs Baker said, then sat down and waited.

He reached for his tape measure. "I need a few measurements, then we'll get started." He led her out to a back room away from prying eyes. He measured everything that could be measured, and even places Millie would never have thought of. "Right, that's done. Follow me out to the main store again."

She'd been so nervous before, Millie hadn't noticed anything. But as she glanced around now she saw the dozens of rolls of materials, all different colors and fabrics. She'd never stepped foot in such a place before today.

It was as nerve wracking as it was exciting.

"So what are we doing for young Millie then?" Joe asked, looking directly at the older woman. She was quite happy about that arrangement as she had no clue.

"She needs at least two ball gowns, and a suit. She'll eventually need something suitable for the Christmas Gala, but we can worry about that later." His smile took up most of his face. "There's a ball next Saturday. Can you have one gown ready by then?"

Saturday? There was a ball next Saturday? Millie's heart fluttered with panic.

"My dear lady," Joe said to Mrs Baker, fully animated, "Anything for Daniel and this sweet lady." It was all Millie could do to stop herself from laughing at his antics.

They walked around the store choosing fabrics, with Joe being given full reign. "For you dear lady, I will make the most beautiful of ball gowns." He reached for a notebook and added a few details. "I can fit you in Thursday at two o'clock for a fitting." He raised his eyebrows at if it was a question. "We can't have you going to the ball in an ill-fitting gown. That would never do." This time he smiled.

"Thursday two o'clock. That will be fine. Thank you." Millie reached out her hand and he took it.

He was still grinning as they left the store.

Chapter Five

"How was your day," Daniel asked as they sat eating supper.

He had a grin on his face, and Millie was sure he already knew. "It was...different. All we did was spend money all day." Her heart sank. She didn't want to be a burden on her new husband, but that's exactly what it felt like.

"Don't look so sad," he said, glancing across at her. "I knew exactly what I was getting into when I sent for a wife." He reached for another biscuit. "These are good," he said, plying it with butter then filling his mouth.

She nodded at the compliment. "I never knew shopping could be so exhausting," she said, buttering her own biscuit.

He laughed, but she couldn't see what was so funny. "At least tomorrow you can rest. Mrs Baker told me you're all set up for the ball – gown, shoes, and matching hat."

She'd never been so spoiled or fussed over in her entire life. Millie wasn't sure she liked it.

"You need to get used to it, Mrs Carson," he said, flippantly, as though he read her mind. "We will attend a lot of functions, and socialize with a lot of important people."

She almost choked on her food.

He frowned at her. "Are you alright?"

She reached for her coffee and took a sip. "Yes. You just caught me off-guard."

"If we'd had time to communicate, you would have known all this." He waved a hand across in front of him. "Never mind. We'll work it out." He reached for another biscuit. "These are really good. You're a wonderful cook, Millie."

Warmth flooded her. At least it was one thing she knew she could do well. "Thank you," she said graciously.

When they'd finished their main meal, she dished out dessert – Cherry Cobbler. It was such a simple dessert to make, but came across as complicated.

As she placed a large portion in front of Daniel, he grabbed her wrist. "You're amazing, Millie," he said, pulling her into his lap. "I never expected any of this, especially after you've had such an exhausting day."

He put his arms around her, and it felt nice. Comforting. She leaned into him, twisting around so she could rest her head on his shoulder.

A feeling of peacefulness came over her. It was as though she'd always been meant to be this man's wife.

The moment the thought entered her mind, guilt consumed her. When Cody was alive, she was deliriously happy. How could she even think that way about her new husband?

Tears welled in her eyes, but she forced them back before Daniel could notice.

"This is nice," he said, totally unaware of her inner turmoil.

She began to pull away, not willing to have these thoughts any longer, but his grip tightened around her waist. "Is everything alright?" He sounded worried, but she dare not face him.

"Perfectly," she said, her face averted. "Eat your dessert while it's still warm. I'll get the clotted cream."

He loosened his grip, and although she felt relieved, she was disappointed at the same time. It had been nice, and she felt comforted – something she hadn't felt since Cody's death.

She didn't know this man, not really, so she put it down to her need for just being held.

They ate the rest of their meal in silence, and Daniel retired to the sitting room while Millie did the dishes and cleaned the kitchen.

He was quietly reading his bible when she entered the room. The warmth from the fire hit her as she entered, and a peacefulness came over her once more.

This was a new feeling for Millie – she couldn't recall having felt this way before. She looked about. There was nothing particularly special about this room that would give her that feeling.

She stared at the beautifully made thickly padded chairs that sat reasonably close to the fire, a small well-made coffee table between them.

The fire was burning, and had a functional screen around it, presumably to protect any children who might visit. Or live there.

The mahogany mantle that sat above it was adorned with two beautifully made candles, with a carved clock sitting between them. At one end was a rather grotesque looking statue, and the other end held two photographs. Who was in those photographs, she had no idea. Perhaps one day she would find out.

Daniel had a bible on his lap, and was reading quietly.

He glanced up, perhaps sensing her presence. "Come in, sit down," he said cheerfully, then went back to his bible.

"Would you mind reading it aloud?"

He glanced up at her, his lips formed a smile. "Most certainly," he said, then began to read.

As the night grew older, and he continued to read, Millie felt a bond building between them. Perhaps they could do this each evening? She would enjoy that, and felt Daniel would too.

He added a bookmark to his well-worn bible, then gently closed it. "It belonged to my grandfather," he said softly. "It's rather worn, but it would have to fall to pieces before I disposed of it."

She could hear the emotion in his voice, and it touched her. One of the few things she had of her parents was their bible. She kept it wrapped in a package of brown paper, and protected by a layer of wool. She hadn't opened it for some years.

Millie fought back the emotion that threatened to overwhelm her. She understood exactly what he was thinking.

"Millie?"

His voice broke through her private thoughts, and she glanced up at him. They were so alike in many ways, and yet so very far apart in others.

"I have my parents bible safely tucked away," she said quietly.

He stared at her momentarily, then spoke gently. "Perhaps one day you'll show it to me?"

She nodded and was more than a little pleased when he didn't pressure her for more information.

He abruptly stood, startling her, then stretched and yawned. "I don't know about you, but I'm tired. Time for bed."

Daniel reached out for her hands and helped Millie to her feet, then pulled her close, slipping his arms around her. She rested her head on his shoulder.

They stood quietly for long moments, and she breathed in his essence, absorbing the tranquility that always seemed to surround him.

"I really like you, Millie," he said suddenly, and she glanced up at him.

"I like you, too."

His arms dropped to his sides, and he began to guide her toward the bedroom. She'd never felt so nervous as right now, heading toward their marital bed.

As though sensing her apprehension, he suddenly stopped. "I suggest we get to know each other better before we have relations," he said gently, and Millie felt relieved.

Getting married was one thing, but consummating a marriage after such a short time was entirely another. "Thank you," she said quietly.

He left the room while she dressed, for which Millie was grateful. Undressing in front of a complete stranger, albeit her husband, was not appealing.

She was already in bed when he returned.

He undressed while she had her back to him and quietly slipped in beside her. The bed moved slightly and she sensed he'd moved closer. His arms crept around her waist, but she didn't flinch. It was somehow comforting.

"Do you mind?" he asked, not at all forcefully.

"Not at all." She liked it, and soon drifted off to sleep.

The night of the ball finally arrived, and Millie was beyond anxious. Daniel could see it in her every action.

He'd finished work at noon, and they'd enjoyed luncheon together.

Her ball gown had arrived Friday afternoon as Joe had promised, and it was beyond beautiful. Millie was a natural beauty, but this gown, it would bring out more of her magnificence. He knew it without even seeing it on her.

When she emerged from the bedroom in her new outfit, he swallowed hard. It was beyond all expectations. Joe had certainly outdone himself this time. The man was well-known for his amazing creations, and transforming women, young and old, into amazing works of art.

"You look...gorgeous," he said, emotion evident in his voice. She stepped toward him, and he wanted to hold her and never let go, but they had to leave. Their carriage was outside waiting.

He helped Millie into her coat, and they were on their way.

He'd attended many of these functions, and found them beyond boring, but they were a necessary evil. Business owners from far and wide attended, and he made contacts he would otherwise miss out on.

He watched as Millie stepped out of the carriage and into the ballroom. Her naivety surrounded her, and her eyes opened wide at the sight before her.

He put his hand to her back, and a thrill went down his spine. He regretted having to remove it to check their coats in at the door.

The band were warming up, and he couldn't wait to get out on the dance floor and show off his beautiful wife.

They took their seats, and it wasn't long before the first course was served. Millie had been quiet, not joining many of the conversations. She was probably overwhelmed.

His biggest client had thankfully been seated on their table, and Mrs Davis, his wife, had taken Millie under her wing. The pair chatted quietly while the men talked business.

The moment Daniel had waited for arrived – the band began to play. They moved onto the dance floor, and all eyes turned to his beautiful wife.

They began with quite the gap between them, but as the music continued, she moved closer. So close in fact, he swore he could feel her heartbeat against his chest. Until finally, her head rested against him, her eyes gently closed.

It felt...intimate. In fact he could honestly say it was the most intimate they'd been since their marriage, and he couldn't say he regretted one moment of it.

The music stopped and she stayed right where she was. He didn't want to move, and apparently, neither did she.

His fingers lifted her chin and she stared up at him. Her eyes glistened and he wondered what was going through her mind. Without thinking, he leaned in and kissed her lips, giving no thought to anyone else or their surroundings.

Daniel didn't want this night to end, and would make the most of each and every dance.

The music began again, and they stayed out on the dance floor. "I'm falling in love with you," he said softly, so only Millie could hear.

She glanced up at him, studying his face. "I feel the same," she told him, and he was shocked but delighted.

He pulled her closer, if that was at all possible.

Tonight was the best night of his life – it could only get better if they consummated their marriage.

Chapter Six

It had been a little over two weeks since the ball, and Millie was deliriously happy.

Daniel was all she could wish for in a husband. He was loving, caring, and gave her all the attention she needed. He was now her husband in every sense of the word.

She set out the mugs for coffee while she waited for the kettle to boil. The bacon was sizzling in the frying pan, and she was about to add the eggs.

Her stomach suddenly twisted and she gagged. Millie stood in the middle of the kitchen in disbelief.

Running toward the bathroom she almost knocked Daniel over in her haste. She was about to lose everything in her stomach, and she hadn't eaten yet!

As her stomach emptied, she couldn't think what could have caused this sudden turn of events. She rinsed her mouth of the foul taste, and splashed her face with water.

Millie stared at her reflection in the mirror. She looked pale, and no wonder. She slapped at her cheeks to put more color into them, then strolled back into the kitchen as though nothing had happened.

"Are you alright?" Daniel looked quite concerned for her welfare. Bless him, he'd finished cooking the breakfast and dished it out. "A little stomach upset. I'm alright now."

He frowned, then nodded and finally ate his breakfast.

As she sat in front of her food, the smell overwhelmed her again, and Millie found herself running to the bathroom once more. Whatever must Daniel be thinking?

"You look awful," he said as she entered the kitchen again. If she still had anything in her stomach, she'd surely be running again, as the odors made her feel completely ill. "A visit to the doctor might be in order," he said, but she refused.

"Perhaps a rest, and I'm certain I'll be fine."

He straightened his tie and put on his jacket. "If you're certain, I'll be off. If it gets any worse, get straight to the doctor." He looked down at her, a worried look on his face.

Millie stood and walked him to the front door. He put on his coat, then pulled her close. She hated that he went to work each day as she missed him so, but loved this time of day where he held her.

She looked up at him and he caressed her lips, ran his hands over her back. "Be well, my love," he said. These last weeks had proven his affection for her, and she'd felt more loved than she'd ever been in her life.

He'd no sooner closed the door than she was running again. It was so draining. Surely she had little left in her stomach to lose?

After emptying her stomach once more, Millie lay down on the bed, more than ready for sleep. She closed her eyes and let her mind rest, and soon she was in a deep slumber.

She was awoken when Daniel sat on the bed next to her. "My poor Millie," he said gently. "I'll call the doctor."

It was the last thing she wanted. "My stomach has settled. It must be some sort of tummy upset." It was then she realized why he was home. "Oh my goodness – you're home for lunch and I've been asleep." She tried to rush to her feet, but he wouldn't let her, holding her back.

"Stay here. I'm more than capable of making a sandwich. What do you think I did before you arrived?" He stroked her cheek lovingly, then headed toward the kitchen.

Despite his words, Millie decided to follow. As she stood, her head spun and she sat down again. *What on earth was going on?*

She sat for a few minutes longer then gingerly stood. This time she was fine. This morning she'd been so unwell, which would likely be the reason behind her dizziness. She decided not to mention it to Daniel, in case he worried.

She strolled into the kitchen as though nothing untoward had happened. He'd found the left-over roast and had made himself a sandwich. The kettle was boiling, so she made him a coffee.

"There are left-over biscuits too if you'd like some," she said, placing a mug in front of him.

He glanced up at her. "That would be lovely." He put his arm around her waist, a worried look on her face. "Are you certain you're alright? I could get the doctor to call in and see you."

She insisted he didn't. It was a one-off thing and she'd be fine by tonight, she was certain of it.

She'd lost too much time sleeping today, and admonished herself. Now supper would have to be some thrown together creation, and she wasn't sure Daniel would like it. He'd had a substantial hot meal every night since she'd arrived. She didn't want to deviate now.

The moment he left she began to chop vegetables for a hearty soup. There was still plenty of time for it to cook. She would cook fried potatoes to accompany the soup, and would make pancakes as well. He surely couldn't complain about that?

She was still feeling a little queasy and nibbled on a slice of toast for her own lunch. Millie didn't feel like more, but was too scared to try anyway.

Once the soup was bubbling on the stove, she lay down again, as she was still feeling poorly. Some time later, her eyes fluttered open. She panicked when she realized her husband would be home in less than an hour.

She took her time standing up, so as not to set off dizziness again. She was pleased when it didn't happen.

Grabbing her apron as she entered the kitchen, Millie went to the stove. The soup was cooking nicely, but needed a stir and perhaps some more salt.

She mixed the flour and milk for the pancakes, then added all the other ingredients. She set it aside for the mix to settle. They were much nicer that way.

The front door opened as she threw the cubed potatoes in the frying pan, and Millie breathed a sigh of relief.

It was then she realized the scent from the food had not bothered her at all.

"How are you feeling," Daniel asked, coming up behind her and kissing her gently on the neck.

She spun around to face him. "I'm fine. No more sickness, but I hate to admit I've slept most of the day."

He frowned. Was he going to admonish her for being so lazy? "You needed it. You look far better tonight." His fingers caressed her cheek and she leaned into his hand.

She reluctantly turned back to the food. "I, I have to do this," she said. "Otherwise it will burn. We'll have soup first, then I'll cook the pancakes." She glanced back at him. "I'm sorry it's not a better meal."

He frowned again. "Please don't keep apologizing. If you were still unwell, I'd have managed." He kissed her forehead then removed his jacket and tie.

She really did win the lottery with Daniel.

Millie was beginning to enjoy having a long soaking bath when she had the time. Daniel didn't seem to mind, and it helped her relax.

Her nausea had returned the past few days, but only in the mornings. She wasn't sure what was setting her off. Whatever it was, she wished it would stop.

She lay back in the tub and closed her eyes. They suddenly flew open. "No! No, no, no!" she said out loud. "It can't be." Tears welled in her eyes and slid down her face. She looked down at her slightly rounded stomach. Why hadn't she thought of this before? It had been the last thing on her mind.

Daniel would be home in a couple of hours. She would soak for just a few more minutes and decide how to tell him, *then* get out. She closed her eyes against the worry.

"There you are. I beginning to wonder if you'd run away."

Her eyes flew open and she looked up to see Daniel standing in the doorway, looking her over.

She screamed.

He laughed.

She tried to cover herself up with her hands, but it was useless. He finally handed her a fluffy white towel. "I have seen you naked before, you know," he said, winking.

She scowled at him. "What are you doing in here? I thought you were at work."

He frowned, then laughed again. "I was, but decided to leave early and spend time with my wife." He looked her over again. "I'm mighty glad I did."

"That is not appropriate, Daniel," she said between gritted teeth, her worry overwhelming her.

The smile left his face. "We are married," he said gruffly, then spun around and stormed out of the room.

She'd offended him. She hadn't meant to, but she had. And now he was upset. Perhaps even angry.

She quickly dried herself, then dressed.

She found him in the sitting room, standing, staring out the window. Was he now sorry they'd married?

Her heart rate increased so much she felt light-headed. "I'm sorry," she said quietly. "You were right. We are married. I...I had no right to yell at you."

He gestured for her to join him. "This is all new to me," he said, wrapping his arms around her waist and pulling her close. "I'm sure it is for you too."

She frowned. He did know she was a widow, right? She'd stipulated the mail-order bride agency tell the potential groom. They'd been married for nearly a month and she was only finding out now?

"Daniel," she said slowly. "I," she swallowed. "I need to talk to you."

He glanced down into her face, then his gaze went lower. Was this gown too revealing? She hadn't thought so until his eyes landed on her cleavage and sat there for a few seconds before roaming back to her face.

At least he had the decency to look embarrassed.

"I made a booking at the diner," he said pointedly. "We need to leave shortly or we'll be late. Get ready and then we'll go."

"But I..."

"You can tell me later." He was insistent, and she eventually gave up and went to prepare for their outing.

This would be one of the hardest things she'd ever had to do. The worst of it was Millie had no idea how he would react. Would he ship her back to where she came from?

If he did, and she was pregnant, not only would she be homeless, she would be a single mother with no means to support her child.

Her heart broke into a million pieces just thinking about it.

~*~

Daniel helped her into her coat. He'd done it a million times before, but this time there was no warmth, no love.

He was still angry with her. Millie swallowed down her disappointment.

She'd never seen him angry before tonight – he'd always been so loving. But she knew this was her fault. Snapping at him like that was not fair. He didn't know of her dismay, had no idea.

Any other time they'd be all over each other, she knew they would.

Despite his anger, he insisted they still go to the diner. It would be nice to see Mrs Baker, and hopefully Daniel would forgive her spur of the moment outburst.

"Good evening, Mrs Baker," he said gruffly, and the older woman turned to Millie and raised her eyebrows. Had she not seen him in this sort of mood before?

It made Millie wonder, but also upset her that she'd caused this anger.

They were led to an isolated table, in the corner, not far from the fire. Daniel said barely a word to either woman.

He helped Millie into her chair, then sat opposite, accepting menus from Mrs Baker. She made herself scarce in record time.

"I'm sorry," she said quietly. "My outburst was unacceptable."

He nodded but said nothing. *Would he never forgive her?*

"Are you ready to order?" Mrs Baker was back in record time. Her eyes moved between them.

Could she feel the tension between husband and wife? Millie decided she could. It almost brought her to tears.

"No. No we're not. Can you give us a minute?" He was not so gruff this time, and Millie felt relief.

Mrs Baker nodded and walked to a nearby table taking orders there.

He reached across the table and covered her hands with his. They were warm and gentle, and she hoped this would be a turning point.

"Daniel, I'm sorry…" she began.

One of the waitresses left a basket of bread in the center of the table, then walked away.

Millie sighed and finally gave up trying to talk to him. She perused the menu before Mrs Baker returned again.

Her guilt was all consuming. It appeared he didn't know she'd been married and widowed, and she desperately needed for him to know.

Especially now.

It was far too late for an annulment, and honestly, she didn't want one. She was too much in love with this wonderful man.

"Have you decided yet?" Daniel glanced across at her at the reappearance of Mrs Baker.

"I should like beef and vegetable soup with warm bread, thank you, Mrs Baker."

Daniel admonished her. "That is not enough. Take another look."

"My, my stomach is still rather churned up," she told her husband. The last thing she wanted or needed was a heavy meal, only to have it emptied in short order.

He nodded. "Of course. You've been rather unwell lately." He reached over and patted her hand. It seemed all was forgiven.

But for how long?

"I'll have the sirloin, thank you Mrs Baker."

She felt herself pale at the mere thought. Mrs Baker's expression was not lost on her.

As she walked away, Millie tried once again to speak with her husband. "Daniel, I really must speak with you. It's important."

He glanced about. "If it really is important, it's probably not something we should discuss here."

She was shattered, but it would have to wait until they were home. The tables were close enough together that any discussions would be overheard. And that was the last thing she needed.

Millie had never been one to lie, or to give false impressions. She wasn't about to start now – she wanted to be upfront with Daniel, and tell him about her previous marriage. And her possible pregnancy.

Millie cried inside. What was she going to do?

"The meal was beautiful. Thank you, Mrs Baker." Millie wiped her lips with the linen napkin and watched as the diner's owner glanced down at her stomach.

She was right. Mrs Baker had guessed at her predicament. Millie put her hands to her stomach defensively, and the woman nodded at her. It was almost like they were best friends keeping a secret between them.

Only she wasn't really a friend. Mrs Baker was an acquaintance who had guessed at her biggest secret. One she hadn't even confirmed for herself, let alone tell her husband about.

Her marriage was doomed.

All she wanted to do right now was curl up into a tight ball and block out the entire world. Especially Daniel.

Her kind and gentle husband who had been nothing but patient with her. Her eyes filled with unshed tears and she turned her head away.

"Daniel, Mr Davis is here with his wife tonight. Why don't you say hello? I'll sit with Millie for a while."

"I can catch up with Mr Davis another time," he said, studying Millie's face.

"Oh look, I think he's waving to you," Mrs Baker said.

"It's fine with me," Millie said quietly, her face still averted.

The moment he was gone, Mrs Baker sat opposite her and reached out. The warmth of her hand was comforting. She watched Daniel's retreating back, and leaned in to listen to the other woman's quiet words.

Chapter Seven

Daniel felt eyes burn into his back as he walked away. It made him feel uncomfortable but was determined not to look back.

When he reached his destination, he was invited to join Mr Davis and his wife, and took every opportunity to glance back toward his table discreetly.

Mrs Baker sat there holding Millie's hand, and it looked as though they were having a heart-to-heart talk.

Millie's head hung low, and she occasionally nodded. She glanced across in his direction and nearly caught him spying on her.

That made him pause. *Was he spying on her?*

He was probably more confused than anything. He was certain Mrs Baker had been trying to get rid of him. But why would she?

"It's good to see you, Daniel," Mr Davis said. "I hear congratulations are in order." He reached out a hand and Daniel shook it.

"We met Millie at the ball, remember dear?" She turned to Daniel. "Where is your bride?" Mrs

Davis stood without waiting for an answer, trying to locate Millie. The moment she did, she was gone, and joined the two women at the table. Mrs Baker put another chair at the table and the three women huddled.

He watched as the two older women patted Millie's hand, then glanced up at him. What was going on? Had he done something to upset her?

His mind rolled back over the day's events. He couldn't think of a single thing, except when he'd spied on her in the bath.

That probably *was* a bit over the top.

"Daniel? I say, you are miles away. Is everything alright?"

Davis and Sons was his best customer, and he was ignoring the man. "I'm wondering what those three are talking about over there." Better to tell the truth, and admit he was not concentrating.

Mr Davis waved a dismissive hand. "Women's stuff. Don't worry about it, Son. One day you'll welcome the reprieve." He laughed, but Daniel couldn't see the funny side.

But he was probably right. Daniel forced himself to concentrate and not worry about the womenfolk who appeared to be talking about him. At the very least the two older women were probably conferring with Millie on how to be a good wife.

He couldn't complain about that.

It seemed like forever before he felt a touch to his shoulder. Mrs Davis sat down and stared pointedly at him. "Millie is lovely, Daniel. You've got yourself a good woman there."

"She certainly is," he said, certain there was something he wasn't being told.

"Whatever happens, you must look after her." She was firm with her words, as though she knew something he didn't.

He frowned and asked himself again, *what was going on?* It was like some massive secret was being shared with other people but not with him.

Did it affect him? He could only presume it did.

He closed his eyes momentarily. Millie had tried to tell him something. Several times. She'd said it was important, but he'd brushed her words aside.

As a result, she'd opened her heart to two much older women who had taken the time to listen. He mentally slapped himself.

What a fool he was.

"Is Millie alright?" He held his breath waiting for her response.

Mrs Davis pursed her lips and stared at him. "You'll have to ask her," she said after several seemingly long moments. And that worried him.

He hurriedly stood, thanked Mr Davis for his company, then left them.

It look far less than twenty seconds to cross the room to his wife, but it felt much longer. Both Millie and Mrs Baker followed his every move. When he had almost reached the table, she patted Millie's hand and left.

His heart skipped a beat. *Was something seriously wrong?*

The closer he got, the more he saw how upset Millie appeared. She was pale – white as baker's flour, and her eyes were red and puffy.

Tonight was meant to be special. A night off for his wife. "Millie?" he said gently as he reached the table. He stood next to her and put an arm around her shoulder.

She glanced up at him. She looked even more upset at this proximity.

Mrs Baker arrived with two serves of Cherry Cobbler and a bowl of clotted cream. "Eat up," she said firmly. "I'll bring you some coffee, Daniel. Tea for Millie." And then she was gone. She had a habit of doing that.

Stupid or not, he asked the question as he sat down. "Is everything alright, Millie?"

She shook her head. He wasn't sure if that meant everything wasn't alright, or she didn't want to talk about it.

More confused than ever, he piled clotted cream onto his Cherry Cobbler, then lifted his spoon and shoveled food into his mouth. That was one way to ensure he didn't say something he would assuredly regret.

He watched as Millie picked at her food then shoved it away. When the beverages arrived, she sipped her tea, then asked to go home.

She was still quite pale.

At the front of his mind was Millie's state of upset and what had caused all this.

He thanked Mrs Baker as they began to leave when he was surprised by her leaning in and whispering to him. "Just listen. Don't interrupt."

He stared at her. She didn't say another word, instead she ran her fingers across her lips in an action that dictated he should zip his mouth. Even more confusion set in, if that was even possible.

Whatever was going on, it was serious. He nodded his acknowledgement and they headed for home.

Had Millie changed her mind? Did she not want to be married to him anymore?

He swallowed hard, and a lump caught in his throat.

It was all his fault, this upset – he'd overstepped the mark by watching her lay naked in the bath, totally without her permission.

He'd enjoyed it in the moment, but it had thoroughly upset her at the time, and she was quite obviously overwrought about it.

As they walked slowly home, her arm hooked through his, he wondered if they'd still be married tomorrow.

Daniel didn't say a word the entire way home.

Neither did Millie. She felt ill, really ill, and worried if she opened her mouth, her supper might come spilling out.

Both Mrs Baker and Mrs Davis had been lovely. They'd calmed her down and given her some practical advise, including that she must tell Daniel without delay.

They insisted he wouldn't send her away. She wasn't convinced.

He didn't know her, not really – she'd been here for less than a month. Despite that, they were madly in love.

They might have said their vows and promised each other forever, but that didn't include accepting and raising another man's child.

She closed her eyes tight, forcing her tears to stay right where they were. She'd done more than enough crying tonight. Made a proper spectacle of herself too.

The older ladies had huddled around her so no one could see. They were friends for life.

If she ended up staying in Grand Falls that was. She stumbled as they reached the bottom of the steps, and Daniel caught her, pulling her close.

He lifted her up into his arms and began to carry her home. "I can walk you know," she said, her voice wobbly. "You can put me down now."

His eyes burned into her, and the reflection from the street lamp played across his face. He clenched his jaw and tightened his grip on her. "I know you're upset, Millie, and I'm truly sorry for what I did to you."

What he did to her?

He continued down the street, still carrying her despite her objections.

"You mean what I did to you?" She hiccupped from trying to hold back her anguish.

"Dear Millie," he said gently. "You did nothing. I behaved like a letch and deserve everything you throw at me."

He unlocked the door, and entered the house, then put her gently to her feet. The movement sent her off-kilter and the room tilted.

He reached out and steadied her.

Almost the moment she was stable, her stomach lurched. She clutched it and ran toward the bathroom.

"Millie?"

She couldn't afford to turn back or he might wear her supper.

After she'd vomited until she could vomit no more, she washed her face with cold water, then rinsed the foul taste from her mouth. It was becoming a habit.

Millie stared at her pale reflection in the mirror. This should be the happiest time of her life, but it had become abhorrent to her.

She fixed her wind-blown hair and made herself more presentable, brushing down the creases from her gown.

"Millie?" Daniel tapped at the door. "May I come in?"

"No." She could only imagine his reaction at her demanding he leave her alone. In his house. "I'll be out shortly."

"As long as you're alright."

Was she? At this very moment Millie thought she was. "I'm fine. I promise."

She heard his footfalls as he returned to the sitting room, and breathed a sigh of relief.

Tonight was going to be difficult – for both of them – but it was something that had to be done.

She couldn't stay beyond tonight if he rejected her. Both Mrs Baker and Mrs Davis offered Millie a roof over her head if it came to that.

Neither woman believed it would, which was a comfort.

She slowly opened the door and headed toward where Daniel was waiting. He turned as she entered the room. "You still look pale," he said, reaching out to touch her cheek.

She pulled out of his reach and he flinched. "I'm sorry," he said, staring at the floor. "I should never had taken my fill of you while you were naked in the bath. It was very wrong of me."

She almost laughed. Is that what he thought?

"Oh no," she said gravely. "This is far worse than that. It is what I have done to you, not the other way around."

He frowned, his confusion evident.

"You've done nothing to me." He stood his ground, and it was gallant, but far from the truth.

"Daniel, sit down. Please."

She began to pace the room, praying her stomach would not churn up yet again.

"Only if you do. You look fair ready to fall over." He guided her to a chair, then sat opposite, studying her face. "You're obviously unwell. I'll call the doctor tomorrow. Tonight if you think it's needed."

She almost laughed at that. *What would the doctor do? Confirm what she believed to be true?*

"I'm sorry," she said more calmly than she thought was possible. "I honestly didn't know. And it's not confirmed so may not be true. But I'm almost certain it is."

He stared at her, confusion written all over his face. It seemed to be his new regular expression. Tonight anyway, and who could blame him? She was babbling, she knew she was.

"Confirm what?" He shook his head. "None of this is making sense. What are you saying, Millie?"

She moved to the edge of her seat and spoke slowly. "What did the mail-order bride agency tell you about me?"

He edged closer. "They sent a telegraph asking if they could send you immediately. Told me your name and age and that it was imperative."

Her heart thundered in her chest. "That was it?"

"Millie," he said urgently. "You must tell me what is going on. Please. You're scaring me."

He was scared? He had no idea how terrified she was right at this minute.

"Daniel," she said gently. "I'm a widow. My husband of only three months was killed two weeks before I arrived here."

He leaned back in his chair, running his hands through his hair. He glanced up at her, but didn't say a word.

"That's not the worst of it," she said firmly. "I think I'm with child," she whispered. Her voice was so low she wasn't convinced he even heard her. "I didn't know, I promise. It's all such a mess." Tears ran down her face.

His head shot up and he suddenly stood. He went to the window and stared out into the darkness.

Her heart felt like that right now – black – with no way out.

After standing there for what seemed hours, he spun around to face her, then rubbed his fingers over the stubble on his chin.

"I guess this changes everything."

Daniel stormed out of the room and headed for the spare room, leaving her to sleep alone and ponder her future.

~*~

Daniel lay under the covers for some hours, but hadn't slept a wink.

He liked Millie, he really did. Loved her in fact. Had he known she was a widow, with a possibility of being with child, he would have said a resounding no to accepting her as his wife.

He squeezed his eyes tight and pondered that thought.

Would he? Would he really have turned her away? A woman in desperate need after falling on hard times through no fault of her own?

It did change everything. The words he'd uttered before storming out of the room were correct, but he didn't need to sound so harsh about it.

It was not Millie's fault she'd found herself in this situation.

His mind went back to his sister, Alison. She was traveling here after her husband was jailed for killing a man in self-defense. But the judge hadn't seen it that way and she'd lost everything, including her marriage.

She'd done what she had to do, and that meant uprooting herself and leaving her husband to rot in jail. Her child was due to be born in little more than two months after her husband's incarceration. He'd lost them both in the accident.

That lump in his throat seemed to grow bigger by the minute.

He threw the covers back and headed to the kitchen in nothing but his drawers, since he'd banished himself to the spare room. His robe and nightgown were in the master bedroom, which he'd effectively handed over to Millie.

As he walked past the room they should be sharing, he heard her stifled sobs. This was all his fault. If he hadn't been so quick to judge, perhaps they wouldn't be in this situation now.

No! They wouldn't be in this situation, that was a certainty. His ego had been damaged and he'd taken it out on Millie.

It wasn't only cruel, it was a dastardly thing to do to anyone, let alone his wonderful wife.

He tapped lightly on the door and the crying stopped. "Millie?" She didn't answer so he opened the door slightly and poked his head around. His heart thudded at the sight before him.

She was curled up into a ball on top of the bed. His heart ached. *He did this to her.* His insides clenched at the thought. "Millie? I'm sorry...I didn't think."

She opened her eyes to look at him briefly then closed them again.

"May I join you?" His heart clenched – he was certain she would refuse him.

Her eyes opened wide, scanning his bare chest this time, then closed again. "It's your bed." She straightened out then climbed under the covers, turning her back on him.

Perhaps that was her way of distancing herself from her half-naked husband.

Did that offend her?

He scooped up his robe and put it on. The last thing he wanted was to offend her more and inadvertently distance them even further.

Daniel wasn't sure what the appropriate action was in these circumstances, but he needed to console his wife, that much was certain.

Laying next to her on the bed, he reached out and touched her cheek. "I'm truly sorry," he said gently. "It was the last thing I expected to hear, and..." He took a steadying breath. "It really threw me."

She nodded, so at least he knew she was listening.

"None of this is your fault." He stroked her hair and she shuffled a little closer to him.

"Would you have taken me if you'd known I was a widow?" Her voice was soft, almost inaudible, and she was obviously still upset.

"Honestly? On the spur of the moment I don't know." His hand stilled. "I'd like to think I would have."

He heard her sigh. Was that a good or bad sign? He had zero experience in these things. Or with women in general. He fervently wished Mrs Baker and Mrs Davis were here to advise *him*. They seemed to have helped Millie.

She slowly turned to face him. "What do we do now? Get an annulment?" Tears filled her eyes and he felt like a heel. "I wouldn't blame you."

Did she think so little of him? That he would evict her because of her situation? A predicament she had absolutely no control over.

Her words cut through his heart and he asked the difficult question. "Is that what *you* want? An annulment?"

Millie shook her head. "Only if you do. I couldn't bear to have you hate me or the baby. An annulment would be better than that."

She rolled over and began to quietly cry again. Daniel slid under the blankets next to her, the cold air finally getting to him. But more, he wanted to be close to her, to comfort her.

He slid his arm around her waist, expecting Millie to push it away, instead she gripped his onto his arm like there was no tomorrow.

Chapter Eight

Millie woke up with Daniel's arm still around her waist. It felt good, but she felt guilty at thinking this way.

Cody had always slept like this, but he'd pulled her much closer to him. His warmth and strong body was always a comfort.

When she'd seen Daniel in only his drawers last night, it had reminded her so much of her lost husband, and her guilt began to eat away at her.

She shouldn't have done this. She should have stayed a widow and not married. No one would have blamed her, but the nagging question was how she would have supported her child.

If she and Daniel got an annulment, that same question would be at the back of her mind. Was at the back of her mind.

What was she going to do?

She slipped out of bed and snatched up her robe, then headed toward the kitchen. She added some fuel to the fire, then filled the kettle.

It was time to start Daniel's breakfast.

She collected eggs and a thick piece of bacon from the pantry. Would she be able to stomach the smell today?

Millie decided to play the good wife until her husband decided to kick her out or organize an annulment. He'd likely do that today.

She sliced enough bacon for the two of them, and threw it in the frying pan with a lump of lard. Daniel entered the kitchen as the smell of cooking food reached her senses.

She almost knocked him over as she bolted.

His eyes burned into her back momentarily, and she hoped he would take care of the sizzling bacon.

Tears filled her eyes as she emptied her stomach. It hurt so much to think she'd come this far only to be sent away again.

What decent man would accept another man's child? There would be an uproar, especially from the women of the town. She'd seen it before. Knew of it first hand.

Her mother had been in a similar situation. Her father – her real father – had taken advantage of her mother, then fled, leaving her in a dire predicament. The man she'd married knew of her situation, and married her regardless.

They'd been childhood friends and he'd loved her from a distance, but stepped up when it mattered. Otherwise Millie would have been handed to her grandmother to bring her up as her own child.

Millie shivered. She was glad that had never happened. Grandmother had always treated her as an outsider.

"Feeling better?" Daniel stood in the doorway, watching her return.

"A little. Until the next round." She stepped into the kitchen and the smell overtook her again.

Daniel frowned. "Is it the smell?" he asked, totally clueless.

"Yes," she yelled, holding her stomach and running.

When she returned, he'd cooked the food and dished it up onto two plates. He'd placed the frying pan in the sink and poured boiling water over it. He'd even opened the window to remove as much of the cooking smells as possible.

That was sweet.

"Thank you," she said, looking around. "But you can't do that every day."

He indicated for her to sit, and placed a mug of tea in front of her. "There's no reason I can't," he said firmly. "At least until you can cope with the smells again."

"And what of the annulment?"

He straightened his back. "Is that what you want?" He suddenly seemed angry.

She took a sip of her tea. "It's far from what I want, but I have to think of you and how this will affect your standing in the community."

His hands fisted at his sides. "You are my wife," he said between gritted teeth. "And I will look after you. Let's hear no more talk of an annulment right now."

Right now? Did that mean it was a possibility down the track? Millie was no better off than she was last night. And she still didn't know whether she would be staying in Grand Falls or being sent away.

She took a small bite of her food and swallowed. It felt like cardboard in her throat. She took a sip of tea to help it down, and looked at her husband over the mug.

The best thing she could do for him was to leave quietly, never to be seen again.

Daniel stared out the window of his office, his heart breaking.

He loved Millie dearly, and he'd behaved abominably to her news. It devasted him to think he'd reacted so badly.

Mrs Francis hovered around, aware something was wrong, but not willing to ask what. She handed him a coffee, then retreated.

It tasted like dirt. *Serve him right.*

He continued to stare, seeing nothing until he spotted Millie walking along the side-walk toward the diner.

He should have know she'd run to Mrs Baker. They seemed to have become quite close. When did that happen?

She turned back and gazed toward his building. His heart clenched at the sight of a suitcase in her hands.

Was she leaving him?

He bolted out the door and ran toward her, not even bothering to grab his coat. Millie was the best thing to happen to him. Since her arrival he'd had joy in his heart again. Before she came, he was simply going through the paces.

She'd made him smile again, gave him a reason to get out of bed. And she'd shown him that money wasn't the only thing worth having.

Love was far more important.

He'd almost caught up when Mrs Baker opened the door to the diner. It was far too early for the diner to be operating, and he frowned.

Had they made a prior arrangement? That set his blood boiling.

He stormed up the steps to the diner and pounded on the door. Mrs Baker peered through the glass at him, indicating he should go away.

He had no intention of leaving. "I want to see my wife," he said gruffly.

She turned her head away and he could hear muffled words but couldn't make them out. When the door was opened, he stormed inside, looking about for his wife.

"I expected better of you than this, Daniel," Mrs Baker said, her tone admonishing.

He couldn't deny the truth of her words – he expected better of himself.

Millie sat near the fire, her head lowered, her hands reaching out for the heat. He slowly made his way toward her, not wanting to appear overbearing.

"Millie," he said quietly.

She looked up at him, but didn't speak. Her eyes were red rimmed, and he knew it was entirely his fault. "Come home. Please?" He was willing to beg her to return home, he loved her so much. "I'm a fool, and we both know it."

She stared at him, not saying a word. Would she ever forgive him?

Mrs Baker interrupted him. "Yes, you are a fool. A far bigger fool than I ever imagined."

She wasn't wrong. "Millie," he said, ignoring the harsh words. "You're my wife. I promise to take care of you and the baby."

She turned away from him and his heart seemed to stop.

"Oh for goodness sakes, Daniel. You're an intelligent man. Say the words Millie needs to hear." She spun around and left them alone.

The words she wanted…. Oh! "I love you, Millie. More than you'll ever know." When she looked at him again, tears were flooding her face. He pulled her into his arms, and he never wanted to let her go again.

Six Months Later...

Millie awoke to the worst pain she'd ever experienced in her life. Daniel's arm was wrapped around her protruding belly as he slept.

"Daniel," she whispered. When he didn't respond she yelled. "Daniel!" He was startled awake. "Get the doctor – I think the baby is coming."

He abruptly sat up and pulled on his breeches. "What can I do?" She almost laughed at his panicked state. She probably would have if she hadn't been in so much pain.

They'd had plenty of time to prepare for this day, but she knew he'd be like this. His calm and collected exterior didn't fool her one little bit.

"Don't forget to tell Mrs Baker on your way back." He propped her up on some pillows trying to make her more comfortable, but nothing was going to work.

She winced and he stared. "Doctor, right. Mrs Baker. Right." He ran in a little circle before he left the room.

Poor Daniel. He'd spent the last few months turning the spare room into a nursery. He'd built a crib, and bought every possible toy he could think of, not to mention more clothes than one baby could ever wear.

Millie had already donated most of them to their local church. She knew they would be very much appreciated by those in need.

Intense pain hit her as she heard the front door open. She prayed it would be Doctor Spencer. Instead Daniel ran in with Mrs Baker close on his heels.

"Put water on to boil, Daniel," she demanded. "Lots of it, then leave."

He looked so forlorn and very defeated. "Where's Millie," she heard the doctor call out from the front of the house.

Daniel showed him in, but refused to go until he'd seen his wife once more. "I love you Millie," he said, kissing her forehead. He wrapped his arms around her, and didn't want to let go. Mrs Baker had to almost wrench him away, then led him to the front door. She could only imagine his demeanor.

If she wasn't in so much pain, Millie would find it amusing.

"Let's prepare you for the doctor, young lady," Mrs Baker said gently. She tucked some folded sheets under her, and removed some of the pillows Daniel had propped her up on.

She watched fearfully as Doctor Spencer pulled out his medical equipment. Mrs Baker blocked her view. "Don't look at him, look at me, Millie," she said quietly. "Birthing a child is not easy, but it will be worth every bit of pain."

She patted Millie's hand, and she felt strangely calm. Until the next pain, when she screamed much louder than before.

"This baby is getting ready to face the world, Millie. Are you ready?" The doctor stared at her then nodded at Mrs Baker, who put an arm around her back and lifted her up slightly.

It was the worst day of Daniel's life. Apart from the day he thought he'd lost Millie.

She was in obvious pain, and there was no way he could help her. He sat on the edge of the sidewalk, his head in his hands.

Fear overcame him. What if he lost her? He knew far too many women had lost their lives giving birth. He shook his head. He couldn't let himself think like that.

He recited his favorite scriptures out loud. That always calmed him, and it did, but he still worried about Millie and the baby.

It had been difficult at first, he admitted it, but he'd accepted this baby as his own. They would bring it up as their own child, and when it was old enough, they'd talk about his or her father. He owed Millie's first husband that much.

One day, they might even have a child of their own. First though, she had to survive her current ordeal.

Daniel couldn't sit around doing nothing any longer. Instead he paced the street, walking past their home, the screams permeating his mind, and would surely fill his nights forever more.

When that didn't appease his sense of concern, he visited the church where they'd married. As he opened the door, Preacher Devon looked up. He walked toward Daniel, his hand outstretched.

"How is Millie doing?" he asked as they joined hands. News got around fast.

Daniel swallowed. "I have no idea. No one is telling me anything."

The preacher indicated for him to sit. "Ah yes, they relegate we poor husbands to the sidelines. Perhaps we could pray for your dear wife and child."

They bowed their heads and the preacher prayed out loud. Daniel's heart clenched at the thought of his darling Millie not surviving. As if he knew what Daniel was thinking, the preacher patted his knee as they prayed.

"Thank you," he said as they walked outside. "I hope our prayers will help."

He left the church and headed toward home. Surely there would some sort of news by now? It seemed to take forever, but he finally arrived and stood staring at the front door. His heart pounded.

Even a small bit of news would help. Dread overcame him the longer he waited. Was Millie even still alive? His heart clenched.

He glanced up as the door opened. "Daniel, come inside," Mrs Baker said gently. "You have a son."

His eyes filled with tears as he sat next to his wife as she cradled their son. "I love you, Millie," he said gently as he hugged them both.

He looked down into the angelic face. He could see so much of Millie in the baby. In the tiny nose, and the sweet lips, and in the fluffy blond hair.

Cody James might not be his natural child, but he would be welcomed into his home. And his heart.

Epilogue

Two Years Later...

Millie sat quietly next to the fire while Cody played at her feet. She cradled ten-month-old Rebecca as she slept.

Daniel stood in the doorway watching over the scene before him. Two and a half years earlier he had no clue this would be his life.

And he didn't regret even a moment of it.

"Papa!" Cody glanced up in delight. He adored his Papa, and was as much Daniel's child as Rebecca was. How could he not accept such a gentle soul into his life?

It was never a question. Well, perhaps in the beginning when he first found out Millie was pregnant to her first husband. But he truly loved Millie, and Cody came along for the ride.

Their very close friends, Mrs Baker and Mrs Davis, knew the truth, but everyone else had assumed the baby arrived early. Which is just the way he liked it.

Daniel would be devasted if Cody was castigated for his heritage.

He leaned in and kissed his wife's cheek, then reached out for the baby. He gently carried her to her crib, and covered her with the precious gifts made by their friends.

Millie stood and stretched on his return. He took her in his arms. He loved this woman more than life itself.

"Did you have a good day," she asked quietly, resting her head on his shoulder.

"I did. And you?"

"We did. We visited Mrs Baker at the diner, and Cody was very well behaved." She grinned down at the boy and he lifted his arms to be cuddled.

Daniel reached down and picked him up, then they had a group hug. "As usual, Mrs Baker spoiled him with a cupcake."

Cody grinned and rubbed his belly. "It was yummy, Papa."

Daniel ruffled his blond hair. "You are far too spoiled, young man," he said in jest.

Millie grabbed his hand, placing it on her belly. His eyes opened in wonderment. Cody's hand sat there too. "Baby," he said, glancing up at his Papa and grinning.

Cody would be the perfect big brother, Daniel was certain. He would look out for his younger siblings, and keep them out of trouble. He was already very protective of Rebecca. If their latest baby was a girl, any prospective suitors had better look out.

Daniel chuckled, and Millie glanced at him. "What's so funny?"

"I was thinking about the future – with Cody as the big brother, protecting his sisters from unsavory young men."

"Whoa. Can we let them grow up first?" She laughed along with Daniel, and he pulled her closer.

Cody ran over to the window and squealed with delight. "It's snowing! Can we build a snowman, Papa? Can we?"

Daniel joined him at the window. "There's not quite enough snow yet, son, but perhaps we can go and cut down a Christmas tree? Just you and me? Mama needs to rest."

Cody jumped up and down and clapped his hands. Daniel loved to make his boy feel special. "I'll change out of my suit, and we'll go. Is that okay, Mama?" He grinned at her. Millie liked to be organized, and hated when he was so spontaneous, but she was getting used to it.

She nodded then left the room to check on Rebecca.

She was getting close to her due date, and would take advantage of the peace and quiet, he was certain.

Daniel walked over to his grandfather's worn and tattered bible and picked it up. He cradled the book, and thanked God for all the goodness He had brought into Daniel's life.

The End

From the Author

Thank you so much for reading my book – I hope you enjoyed it.

Cheryl's other books in this series are:

Mail Order Hannah
Mail Order Pearl

About the

Author

Multi-published, best selling and award-winning author, Cheryl Wright, former secretary, debt collector, account manager, writing coach, and shopping tour hostess, loves reading.

She writes both contemporary and historical western romance, as well as contemporary romance and romantic suspense.

She lives in Melbourne, Australia, and is married with two adult children and has six grandchildren.

When she's not writing, she can be found in her craft room making greeting cards.

Author Links

Website: *http://www.cheryl-wright.com/*

Blog: *http://romance-authors.com/*

Facebook Reader Group:
https://www.facebook.com/groups/cherylwrightauthor/

Join My Newsletter:

https://cheryl-wright.com/newsletter/